A NOTE FROM THE AUTHOR

Sailing away on our ship, through the living room to Treasure Island, is a childhood memory which still makes me tingle with happiness. My brother and I braved the choppy seas and kept a lookout for those pesky pirates through our cardboard telescopes, while Dad provided much amusement as the Loch Ness Monster. Quite what the Loch Ness Monster was doing in the shark infested ocean I never knew.

Jess Mikhail draws the pictures

© Susannah Tomkins

Eva Katzler writes the stories

There was always something about the concept of hidden treasure which captured my imagination and set me spinning off into a world of sea adventures.

Pirate flags, treasure maps, telescopes and shanty singing at the tops of our voices featured heavily in our make-believe land. Pirate hats and eye patches were worn with pride and, with our parents leaping into character as well, being at home on a rainy day became the most exciting prospect in the world.

Florentine and Pig is a safe, imaginative and fun-filled world, which encourages families to read, play and create together. It celebrates the imagination of little ones and champions parents' loving and creative relationships with their children.

All the recipes and crafts in this book have been designed for children to make with help from a responsible adult, so grab your aprons and sticky tape and jump on board!

Eva X

© Gem Pope

Recipes and crafts by Jess and Laura Tilli

For more recipes, crafts and ideas, please pop over to **www.florentineandpig.com** or become our fan on Facebook — we'd just love to see you there!

Remember, sharp knives and hot things can be dangerous.
Adults should supervise children closely when cooking and crafting.

For Christine, the bravest and most adventurous pirate I know – EK

For my playmates, Rowan and Christine, who made
my childhood very special and a tiny bit bonkers x – JM

Bloomsbury Publishing, London, New Delhi, New York and Sydney

First published in Great Britain in 2013 by Bloomsbury Publishing Plc
50 Bedford Square, London, WC1B 3DP

Text copyright © Florentine and Pig Ltd 2013
Illustrations copyright © Jess Mikhail 2013
Recipes devised and crafts co-devised by Laura and Jess Tilli
Wallpaper design reproduced by kind permission of Elanbach
The moral rights of the author and illustrator have been asserted

A CIP catalogue record for this book is available from the British Library

ISBN 978 1 4088 3020 8 (HB)
ISBN 978 1 4088 2440 5 (PB)
ISBN 978 1 4088 2940 0 (eBook)

1 3 5 7 9 10 8 6 4 2

Printed in China by C&C Offset Printing Co Ltd, Shenzhen, Guangdong

www.bloomsbury.com
www.florentineandpig.com

Florentine and Pig

and the
Lost Pirate Treasure

Eva Katzler

Illustrated by Jess Mikhail

Recipes and crafts by Laura and Jess Tilli

BLOOMSBURY

LONDON NEW DELHI NEW YORK SYDNEY

'Oh, Pig!' exclaimed Florentine as she leapt out of bed. 'Today is a playing-outside day and I cannot **wait** to go out in the sunshine!'

Pig ran to the window and peeked behind the curtains.
Then he looked at Florentine and wrinkled his nose.

'Whatever's the matter, Pig?' asked Florentine. 'Isn't it a beautiful day
with a sparkling blue sky and aren't the birds singing happy bird songs?'

FLORENTINE

PIG

Pig flung open the curtains
and Florentine gasped.
'Oh, Pig!'

There was a loud **rumble** of thunder,
a **crash** of lightning, and big drippy drops
of soggy splashy rain were tumbling
down all around.

'What a terribly gloomy day,'
said Florentine glumly.

Pig shivered and nodded.

'Come on, Pig, let's put on our cosiest things and keep out of the cold,' said Florentine.

Florentine and Pig delved into their chest of Wintry Warm and Cosy Things. There were . . .

scarves and socks,
jumpers and jackets,
gloves and galoshes . . .

and a rather peculiar-looking **hat**.

'Oh, Pig, you do look funny,'
Florentine giggled as she put on her
very favourite cosy cardigan with the
three big Ever-So-Sparkly Buttons.

But . . .

Missing!

'Oh NO, Pig!' Florentine cried.
'One of my Ever-So-Sparkly Buttons
is missing!'

They searched **high** and **low**.

They searched **under** and **over**.

They searched **beside** and **between**.

But the Ever-So-Sparkly Button
was nowhere to be seen.
'Oh dear,' said Florentine.
'What **are** we going to do?'

Pig held up his telescope.

'You're right, Pig,' said Florentine. 'We are going to have to sail to the **Lost Treasure Island** to find my Ever-So-Sparkly Button.'

They set their sail and checked their Crow's Nest.

They shoved in their shovels . . .

and, last of all, they marked their map.

Pig fetched their hamper.
'Good idea, Pig,' said Florentine.
'We don't want to get hungry on our sea voyage!'
They darted about the kitchen making delicious things to eat.

'Goodness me, Pig!' Florentine exclaimed. 'You're so speedy!'
Pig really could move rather quickly when he put his mind to it.

Soon the hamper was filled to the very top.
What a scrumptious lunch they would have!

Florentine and Pig's Lost Pirate
Treasure Recipes

★ 'Aye Aye' Cheesy Mashed Potato Rollies

★ Blueberry and Yoghurt Treasure Chest Cakes

★ 'X Marks the Spot' Sparkle Cookies

★ 'Yo Ho Me Hearties' Beans on Toasties

★ 'Ooooo Arrrrr' Pirate Pasta

★ Ginger and Honey Hot Choc Grog

with Marshmallow Jewels

'Come on, Pig,' said Florentine. 'It's time to go!'
Pig jumped aboard and they were off! They sailed away
on the ocean towards the Lost Treasure Island.

'Isn't it exciting!' said Florentine.
'I do hope we find my
Ever-So-Sparkly Button.'

Florentine and Pig saw wild white seagulls squawking, pretty pink fish flapping and sparkling silver dolphins diving but there was still no sign of the Lost Treasure Island.

'Do you think we might be lost, Pig?' asked Florentine worriedly.
'Might we have taken a **wrong turn?**'

Pig peered through his telescope.
Up, down, left and right . . .

. . . and then a grin spread across his face. For there, straight ahead, was the Lost Treasure Island!
Florentine clapped her hands together excitedly.

'Oh, Pig! We did it! How marvellous!'

Florentine and Pig anchored their boat, grabbed their shovels, jumped on to the Lost Treasure Island and started to hunt.

They searched **high** and **low**.

They searched **under** and **over**.

They searched **beside** and **between**.

But the Ever-So-Sparkly Button was **nowhere** to be seen.

'Oh, **Pig**,' said Florentine sadly.
'What **are** we going to do?'

Pig grabbed the hamper.

'Good idea!' said Florentine.

'Let's have lunch!'

They **gobbled** and **guzzled**.

They **chewed** and **chomped**.

They **crunched** and **munched**.

What a delicious lunch!

'We'd better sail home before it gets dark,'
said Florentine. 'We don't want to get lost, do we, Pig?'

'Goodbye, Lost Treasure Island!' cried Florentine as they waved.
'Oh, Pig, I **am** sad that we didn't find my Ever-So-Sparkly Button,' she sighed.

Just then, something under the water caught Pig's eye.
Something very shiny.
Something very sparkly.

Suddenly there was a big splash and Pig was gone!

'PIG!' cried Florentine. 'Where are you?!'

There was a **splatter**

and a **gurgle**
and a **splutter.**

And suddenly there was a very soggy Pig clutching an
Ever-So-Shiny, Ever-So-Sparkly . . . Button!

Sparkly
button

'Oh, Pig, you ARE clever,'
cried Florentine. 'You found it!'
Pig did a little dance.

'What a wonderful adventure' said Florentine.
'I do hope it rains again tomorrow . . .'

The End...Ta da

'Aye Aye' Cheesy Mashed Potato Rollies

Makes 6

You will need

2 big potatoes (skins on), chopped up, boiled and drained

1 small handful grated cheese

3 spring onions, chopped into small bits

1 handful chopped parsley

1 packet ready rolled puff pastry

1 free range egg, beaten

Butter and milk, enough to squish with

Salt and pepper

Poppy seeds to sprinkle

1. Preheat your oven to 180°C/350°F/Gas Mark 4.

2. Put the potatoes into a bowl with a splodge of butter and a splash of milk. Mash away until nice and smooth but not too wet. Mix in the cheese, spring onions, salt, pepper and parsley.

3. Lay the puff pastry onto a floured surface and cut in half, lengthways. Take half of your potato mixture and make a long sausage shape right down the middle of one of your pieces of pastry.

4. Using a pastry brush or your fingers, brush the beaten egg onto both edges of the pastry then wrap the pastry tightly around your potato sausage and turn over so the join is on the bottom. Do the same with the rest of your mixture and your other piece of pastry.

5. With a table knife, cut both potato sausages into 6 pieces and make two slits in the top of each rollie, so that the steam can escape. Brush a little more egg on the top and sprinkle with poppy seeds.

6. Place on a baking tray and bake in the oven for about 25 minutes or until you can see your rollies turning a golden brown colour. Delicious served with yummy pickle!

Blueberry and Yoghurt Treasure Chest Cakes

For the chests

150g caster sugar
150g soft butter
2 free range eggs, whisked
225g self-raising flour
125g blueberries
2 tbsp natural yoghurt
1 tsp baking powder

For the treasure

200g butter
400g icing sugar, plus extra for sprinkling
1 tbsp water
100g blueberries
1 small handful chocolate raisins
1 small handful dried apricots, chopped

1 Preheat your oven to 180°C/350°F/ Gas Mark 4.

2 In a big bowl, mix together the butter and sugar with a wooden spoon until nice and creamy. Add the eggs and yoghurt and mix again.

3 Tip in all the flour, baking powder and 125g blueberries and mix really well. Line the cake tray with the cake cases and, using two teaspoons, dollop two big spoonfuls of the mixture into each cake case.

4 Pop them into the oven for 20 minutes or until they are springy to touch and golden brown, then leave them to cool on a wire rack. Once cooled, take them out of their wrappers and carefully slice the tops off. Keep these to one side.

5 Mix the butter and icing sugar together until smooth, then dollop a spoonful onto each cake. Stick the blueberries, apricots and raisins into the icing and replace the cake tops. Use a sieve to sprinkle over the icing sugar . . . share with only your most treasured pirate friends.

'X Marks The Spot' Sparkle Cookies

Makes
12

You will need

100g dark chocolate
100g milk chocolate
175g soft brown sugar
2 free range eggs
25g butter
85g flour
Edible glitter

1 Preheat your oven to 180°C/350°F/Gas Mark 4.

2 Rest a bowl over a pan of simmering water and gently mix the chocolate and butter together until it's all melted and shiny.

3 In another bowl, mix together the eggs, sugar and flour with a wooden spoon. Pour in your chocolate mixture and mix again.

4 Using two spoons, splodge 6 circles of your mixture onto the lined baking tray. Bake 6 at a time so they have room to spread. Pop into your hot oven for 12-15 minutes.

5 Transfer to a wire rack to cool. While the cookies are still warm, use the back of a knife to make a big X shape on each and sprinkle with your sparkly glitter!

Shiver Me Timbers Pirate's Flag!

You will need
A stick from the garden
A rectangular piece of card
Black water-based paint
Sticky tape
Felt tip pens

1. On a flat surface, lay the stick onto one end of the card. Fold the card over the stick and tape it down to keep in place.

2. Squash your hands into the black paint and make handprints at the bottom of the card.

3. Using your finger make the skull, eyes and mouth.

4. Decorate with felt tip pens.

Swashbuckling Pirate's Hat

You will need

Long thin strip of card (about 4cm high) that fits around your head
Large piece of black card
White buttons, small bits of white paper or tin foil, and other sparklies
Glue stick
Stapler
Scissors

1 Carefully cut a pirate hat shape out of the black card and lay flat on a table. Glue along the straight edge.

2 Stick the long, thin piece of card to your gluey edge, making sure you have enough card each side to wrap around your head.

3 Turn your hat over and use glue to stick your buttons or pieces of paper/foil all over your pirate's hat to make it sparkle and shine.

4 Once the glue is dry, wrap your thin piece of card around your head and ask a grown up to secure it in place with a stapler.

'Yo Ho Me Hearties' Beans on Toasties

You will need

4 slices granary bread

Butter for spreading

1 tin baked beans

1 small onion, chopped into small pieces

1 small handful grated cheddar cheese

1 small handful of frozen peas

1 spring onion, cut into tiny pieces

1 squirt of tomato ketchup

Salt and pepper

1 tbsp olive oil, for frying

6 wooden skewers

1 Put the olive oil into the frying pan with the onion and the spring onion, and sizzle until soft. Add the baked beans and peas and stir well using a wooden spoon. Cook until it's bubbly and hot, then take off the heat.

2 Mix in the cheese, ketchup and a sprinkle of salt and pepper.

3 Toast the bread and spread it with butter. Lay out two pieces of your toast and put a big spoonful of the hot, cheesy bean mixture onto each. Make sure you spread it out – don't miss the corners! Now put the two other pieces of toast on top to make two bean toasties.

4 Cut each sandwich into four triangles and stack four on top of each other, using the wooden skewer flag poles to secure your pirate flag stacks. (You can even make a flag for your pole out of scrap paper!)

'Oooo Arrrr' Pirate Pasta

Makes 6

You will need

300g wholewheat pasta

12 cherry tomatoes, halved

1 tin chopped tomatoes

2 spring onions, snipped into chunks

8 fish fingers

1 small handful grated cheddar cheese

1 handful fresh basil leaves, torn up

1 tub cress

1 tbsp olive oil, for frying

1. Preheat the grill to a medium heat.

2. Line up the fish fingers on the baking tray and grill for about 7 minutes on each side, or until they are cooked through.

3. Fill the big saucepan with boiling water from the kettle and carefully tip in your pasta. Boil and bubble for about 20 minutes, or until the pasta is soft, then drain and put back into the pan.

4. Put a glug of olive oil into the frying pan along with the cherry tomatoes and spring onions and sizzle for 5 minutes. Add the tinned tomatoes and fresh basil, and bubble until piping hot.

5. Tip the tomato mixture into the pasta pan and stir. Snip the fish fingers into chunks with scissors and add to the pasta. Stir gently.

6. Pour the pasta into your bowls and sprinkle over your cheese. Add the cress on top by snipping with scissors. Dive in!

Ginger + Honey Hot Chocolate Grog with Marshmallow Jewels

Makes 6

You will need

800ml milk, and extra for dipping
200g milk chocolate
3 tbsp cocoa, and extra for
  dipping and sprinkling
2 tsp ground ginger
1 tbsp runny honey
1 large handful of marshmallows

1 To give your mugs a chocolatey rim, pour a little milk into one saucer and put 3 tablespoons of cocoa on to another. Take each mug and dip the rims first into the milk and then into the cocoa.

2 Break the chocolate into chunks and melt in a bowl over a pan of simmering water, until it's nice and shiny.

3 Put all your remaining ingredients, apart from the marshmallows, into the big saucepan and whisk together over a gentle heat. Swirl in the melted chocolate.

4 When the grog is bubbling at the edges, ladle it into your cocoa rimmed mugs.

5 Add the marshmallow jewels, sprinkle over a little extra cocoa and you're ready for a piratey shindig!